# The NEW Small Person

## Lauren Child

To
Beatrice
and
Angelica
love
from
Lauren

PUFFIN BOOKS    Published by the Penguin Group: London,
New York, Australia, Canada, India, Ireland, New Zealand and South Africa
Penguin Books Ltd, Registered Offices: 80 Strand, London WC2R 0RL, England

puffinbooks.com    First published 2014    001
Text and illustrations copyright © Lauren Child, 2014
Made and printed in China
Hardback ISBN: 978-0-141-38491-7
Paperback ISBN: 978-0-723-29361-3

Elmore Green started off
      life as an only child,
as many children do.
He had a room all to himself,
and everything in it was his.

He was very proud
       of his room.

He watched all his favourite cartoons on his own little TV set – no one ever changed the channel.

He could line up all his precious things on the floor and no one moved them ONE millimetre.

When his Uncle Cecil gave him a jar of jelly beans,
Elmore could eat every single bean, all by himself –
in whatever order he liked.

There was no worry about anyone
eating the orange ones because
Elmore Green's parents

did NOT

eat

jelly beans.

Elmore Green's parents thought he was simply the funniest, cleverest, most adorable person they had ever seen.

And Elmore Green liked that because it is nice to be the funniest, cleverest, most adorable person someone has ever seen.

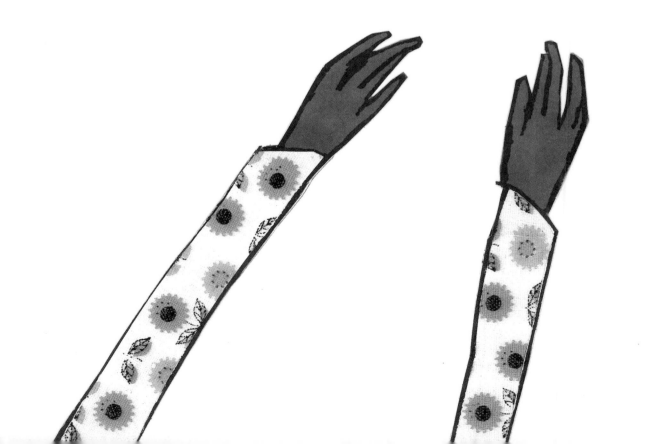

But
then
one day
everything
changed.

Somebody else came along.

The new person was small
and didn't do much but still
people picked it up
and smiled at it
and gave it things to chew.

They all seemed to
like it . . .

maybe

a little bit

MORE

than

they

liked

Elmore Green.

The new small person didn't like watching
Elmore Green's favourite TV cartoons
and would

**squawk**

until the channel
was changed.

Elmore did NOT find shows
for small people at all stimulating.

But everyone said
the small person
couldn't help it
because it was
ONLY
small.

Sometimes the small person would come
into Elmore's room and knock things over
and sit on things that didn't want to be sat on.

Once it actually licked Elmore's jelly bean collection,
including the orange ones. As anyone knows,
jelly beans that have been licked
                                    are NOT nearly
                                    so nice.

But
everyone    said    Elmore

could NOT be cross because the small person was ONLY small.

Elmore Green wished
the small person
would go back to
wherever it
came from.

But
Elmore's
parents
explained
that this
was NOT
possible.

# The small person got bigger.
And things got much worse.

One day Elmore found the small person
wearing his fourth most favourite outfit.
Without asking.

"That's mine," said Elmore.
"It is NOT for small people."

"I want to be the same as YOU,"
said the small person.

But Elmore Green
did NOT want to be
the same as
someone
small.

The small person
followed
Elmore Green
everywhere.

It wanted to sit
next to him, it wanted to
copy everything that Elmore did,
it wanted to be everywhere
that Elmore was.

"Where are you going Elmore?"
said the small person.

"Nowhere," said Elmore.

"Can I come?" said
the small person.

When the small person
said things like this,
Elmore Green would go
and sit up a tree.

He
did
NOT
want
someone
small   following him around.

One awful day
the small person
    moved its bed into
Elmore Green's
        room.

Now Elmore couldn't get away from it.
        It was always there looking at him.

    Sometimes it would stretch out
            its arms and say, 'Huggle!'

But Elmore didn't want t

cuddle up to someone small. However, one night everything changed.

Elmore Green had a BAD dream. It was very upsetting —
a scary thing was chasing him, waving its grabbers
and GNASHING its teeth.

Elmore screamed and the small person
bravely got out of bed and
clung on to him.

"Go away Scary!" shouted the small person.

It was nice
to have someone there
in the dark when
the scaries were about.

A few days later Elmore Green was lining up all his
precious things so they reached from his bedroom door
to all the way down the stairs.
It was a very long line of things.

The small person was very amazed. "Oooh," it said.

"I could make them reach to the front door
if I had more things," said Elmore.

"I have more things," said the small person.
"I have at least five or three things.
You can have them."

It felt good to have
someone there who understood
why a long line of things
was so
special.

The next evening Elmore was laughing at the TV.

The small person looked at Elmore and then
at the TV and then he laughed TOO.
    It was very funny.

More funny
somehow
with TWO people
laughing than just ONE.

Elmore opened his jar of jelly beans.
"You can have a jelly bean
if you like, Albert."

His brother, Albert, smiled.
Elmore smiled back.

"Whichever
colour
YOU like . . ."
said Elmore.